Zombies
Don't
Play Soccer

There are more books about the Bailey School Kids!
Have you read these adventures?

Zombies Don't Play Soccer

by Debbie Dadey
and
Marcia Thornton Jones

illustrated by John Steven Gurney

A
LITTLE APPLE
PAPERBACK

SCHOLASTIC INC.
New York Toronto London Auckland Sydney

ISBN 0-590-22636-3

22 21 20 19   23/0

Printed in the U.S.A.   40

First Scholastic printing, September 1995

Book design by Laurie Williams

For Brantly David Rosenfeld
— MTJ

For Scott, Neil, and Mark Dadey
— DD

With special thanks to Nathan Leigh Dadey,
for technical advice.

Contents

1
Practice

"We don't need a new coach," Eddie complained and kicked his soccer ball hard. "Coach Ellison is the best soccer coach we've ever had!"

"How can you say that?" Liza asked as she walked onto the soccer field with her two friends, Eddie and Howie. "We haven't won a single game this year."

"Eddie just likes Coach Ellison because he lets Eddie goof off," Howie told her.

Eddie smiled and kicked his soccer ball again. "Goofing off is what I do best," he said.

"Coach Ellison probably gave up soccer for good after what you did to him last week," Melody said as she came on to the field and kicked the ball back to Eddie.

"What did I do?" Eddie asked innocently.

Howie sat down to put on his shin guards and looked at Eddie. "Don't you remember putting vinegar in his water bottle?" Howie asked.

Liza plopped down beside Howie. "Eddie does so many rotten things, he can't remember half of them," Liza said.

"I remember," Eddie said, laughing and kicking the ball at the same time. "Coach Ellison's face looked like a sick pug dog's. He spit that vinegar at least fifteen feet. He must have set a world's record for distance spitting."

"He also set the world's record for getting us a new coach," Melody reminded him as she picked up the ball.

Eddie shrugged. "Maybe it's about time we had a soccer coach that will help us Bailey Boomers win."

Melody pointed her finger at Eddie. "To win, you have to work hard. If this new coach works us to death, it'll be your fault."

"Don't be so dramatic," Eddie told her. "No coach is going to work a bunch of third-graders to death."

Just then the kids heard a loud bellowing from across the field. "Get your out-of-shape, lazy bodies over here. We're going to practice until we drop. Move it!" the voice screamed. "Move it!"

Eddie looked at his friends. "Of course, I could be wrong about the working to death part."

Liza started running. "Eddie," she gulped, "what have you gotten us into?"

2
The New Coach

"Oh, no!" Eddie stopped short before they got to the practice area. "The new coach is a woman!" The four kids stopped and stared. A very tall woman with wide shoulders and a sweatband around her head was bouncing a soccer ball up in the air with the side of her foot. The front of her T-shirt read *Coach*.

"What's wrong with a woman soccer coach?" Liza asked.

Eddie pulled his baseball cap off his head and slammed it on the ground. "She probably doesn't know anything about soccer. We'll have to tiptoe around the ball so we don't break her fingernails."

Melody threw the soccer ball right at Eddie's stomach. He barely had time to sidestep it. "Girls can do anything boys can do," Melody said. "And don't forget that I've made more goals than anybody on the team."

"Just because you're good, doesn't mean . . . " Before Eddie could complain any more a big hand grabbed him by the shoulder. Eddie had to look way up to meet the eyes of their new soccer coach. She was tall, but what were really big were her shoulders. Most professional football players didn't have shoulders that wide, even with their shoulder pads on.

"Hi," Eddie squeaked.

"Hi, there," the new coach roared. "Do you plan on growing roots or playing soccer?"

"Soccer," Melody said loudly.

"Then let's get practicing!" the coach yelled. All the other kids on the team cheered.

"Excuse me," Liza raised her hand and asked softly. "Are you the new coach?"

The huge lady pointed to the sweatshirt she was wearing.

Liza nodded and sniffed like she was about to cry. "Yes," Liza said, "but I wondered what your name is."

"My name is Graves," the huge lady bellowed. "That's Coach Graves to you. I came all the way from New Orleans to coach your soccer team. The game is exciting enough to wake the dead!"

"We may be dead after playing for her," Eddie whispered.

"Enough talking," Coach Graves snapped. "Let's see how much soccer you know."

Coach Graves had the Bailey Boomers twisting and turning. They kicked and they dribbled. They ran and they passed. Coach Graves cheered when they did something right. She yelled directions when they goofed up. She had to yell directions a lot. At the end of an hour sweat was pouring off every kid.

"Remember to work together!" Coach Graves hollered as they got ready to leave. "You need teamwork to win games! Work together! Practice teamwork!"

Eddie wiped sweat from his forehead. "I don't need teamwork to win. I don't even need a woman coach!"

"Shhh," Melody warned. "She'll hear you."

But it was too late. Coach Graves frowned at Eddie as the team walked off the field.

"Well," Liza panted when they were away from the coach, "I hope you're happy, Eddie. This new coach is your fault. I'm dead on my feet!"

Eddie giggled and made his arms and legs stiff. Then he started coming after Liza. "I'm the walking dead!"

Melody took a drink of water. "You shouldn't joke about dying."

But Eddie was too busy chasing Liza to hear. Liza shrieked and raced across the empty field.

3
Winning Season

Melody threw her drink bottle at Eddie. Ice cold water splashed him in the face. "Argh!" Eddie cried, "What did you do that for?"

"I wanted to bring you back to life." Melody giggled.

Eddie wiped water off the end of his nose and frowned. "I'm half drowned now."

"Don't be such a baby," Melody told him. "Everyone's tired, but if we want to win games, this new coach is just the one to help us."

Howie nodded. "Melody's right."

Liza rubbed her legs and groaned. "I think I'd rather lose than suffer like this."

"It'll be worth it, if we win a few games," Melody told her.

"A few games?" Eddie shouted. "With this kind of practicing, we're going to beat every team in the state, even the Sheldon Shooters!"

Howie, Liza, and Melody smiled. The Sheldon Shooters were the best soccer team around. Every year they won game after game.

"Do you really think we stand a chance against the Shooters?" Liza asked.

"Sure," Eddie said. "The Bailey Boomers will be number one!"

"Thanks to Coach Graves," Melody reminded them. The four kids looked over to the sidelines. Coach Graves was still there. Standing beside her was an old woman.

"That lady looks like a reject from an old-time horror movie," Eddie said.

Melody shivered, "She gives me the willies." The old woman had long stringy hair that hung over her wrinkled face. Her black dress almost reached the ground.

"We really shouldn't stare at her," Liza said. "She can't help it if she's old."

"And you can't help it if you're a wimp," Eddie said.

Liza tossed her water bottle at Eddie. "You can't help it if you're all wet."

The kids laughed, but they got very quiet when they saw the old woman making big circles in the air with her gnarled

hands and yelling at the coach.

"Maybe we'd better get out of here," Howie whispered. Just then, the old woman pointed at the kids and laughed.

"Let's go!" Melody screamed. "Before it's too late!"

4
The Argument

Melody ran all the way to a big clump of bushes and hid behind them. Liza, Howie, and Eddie piled in beside her.

"For someone so tired, you sure run fast," Howie told her. "What's wrong?"

Melody peered over the top of the bushes toward the old woman and Coach Graves. They were busy talking to each other. "Didn't you see the way that old lady looked at us?" Melody asked her friends. "It was like she was casting a spell."

Eddie shook his head. "I think she was laughing at how we play soccer."

"Then why was she yelling at Coach Graves?" Howie asked.

Melody peered over the bushes again. "All I know is that there is something very scary about that old woman, and I don't think it's safe to be around her."

"You're the scariest person I know," Eddie told her, "but I hang around you all the time."

"Shhh," Howie said, looking over the bushes. "Maybe Melody's right about that old woman. She's really giving it to the coach."

All of the kids lifted their heads slowly over the top of the lilac bushes. They could see the old lady shaking her fist at Coach Graves.

"She's yelling at the coach," Melody said.

Howie put a finger to his lips. "Be quiet so we can hear her."

The old lady's words echoed over the field. "Come with me now!"

Coach Graves shook her head.

"Come with me," the old lady said again, "or you will be sleeping here forever!"

"Don't threaten me," Coach Graves said.

The old woman smiled, showing a broken tooth. "You should know by now, I don't threaten. I make promises."

Coach Graves shook her head again. "I'm not going anywhere. I'm going to stay right here in Bailey City and coach soccer."

"Stay here then," the old woman cackled and made strange motions with her hands. "But you will be sorry." The kids shivered and quickly ducked their heads down when the old woman turned toward them. "You will be sorry," she said. "You will all be sorry!"

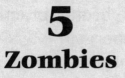

5
Zombies

Melody, Howie, and Eddie waited for Liza under the oak tree on the Bailey Elementary playground. The tips of the giant tree's leaves were just starting to turn yellow. It was early Saturday morning, and the four friends were going to soccer practice. Liza skipped across the playground to meet her friends.

"Phe-ew!" Eddie squealed through a pinched nose. "You smell like a dead skunk!"

Liza put her hands on her hips and glared at Eddie. "I'm ready for a killer soccer practice. Mom let me use some muscle ointment."

"I wish I'd thought of that," Melody said as they headed for the soccer field on the other side of the playground. "I bet Coach Graves is ready and waiting with another brutal practice. She sure has a lot of energy."

Howie pointed to the bleachers on the far side of the field. "It looks like she got tired of waiting."

Howie was right. Most of the other players were already clustered around a goal, but Coach Graves acted like she didn't even see them. She sat very still on the bleachers, holding the soccer ball on her lap.

"It looks like she's sleeping," Melody said.

Eddie shook his head. "She can't be sleeping. Her eyes are wide open." The four friends looked where Coach Graves was staring.

"What is she looking at?" Liza asked.

Howie shrugged. "She's just staring into space. A lot of people do that when they're thinking. Let's tell her we're ready to play." Howie led his friends down the

sidelines of the playing field and stopped right in front of Coach Graves. He waited for her to notice him, but she didn't even blink.

Howie cleared his throat. "We're ready to play soccer, Coach."

Coach Graves didn't move, except to nod one time.

"We need the ball," Melody blurted.

Coach Graves let go of the ball. It rolled off her lap and bounced to the ground, landing near Eddie's dirty sneakers. Eddie sent the ball flying to the middle of the field with a mighty kick. *Whack!*

All the Bailey Boomers chased after it. Melody got to the ball first. She dribbled it down the field without letting anyone else near it. A fat boy named Huey tried, but he ended up bumping into Howie instead.

Eddie listened for Coach Graves to blow her whistle and yell directions, but she didn't. He glanced at the sideline.

Coach Graves still sat on the bleachers, staring into space. Eddie grinned. It didn't bother him one bit that Coach Graves wasn't paying attention. Eddie wasn't a great soccer player, but there was something else he was good at — trouble.

The first thing he did was trip Melody. He glanced over his shoulder as he took off after the ball. Coach Graves acted like she hadn't seen a thing. Eddie tried to kick the ball, but he missed. So he scooped the ball up with his hands.

"Hey!" Liza yelled. "No hands allowed!"

Eddie tucked the ball under his arm and raced down the field to make a goal. Then he pranced around in a victory dance.

"That's cheating," Howie gasped when he caught up with him.

Liza nodded. "You're not playing by the rules!"

"Neither was Melody," Eddie argued.

"She wasn't letting anybody else near the ball."

Melody took a step closer to Eddie. "That's because nobody else is good enough to get it from me."

"We'd play better if you shared with the team," Huey called out. That started everybody arguing. Melody yelled at Huey, and Howie snapped at Eddie. Liza tried to get everybody quiet, and Eddie just stood there grinning.

"*Quiet!*" Liza screamed. "We shouldn't be fighting like this!" The Bailey Boomers fell silent. They'd never heard Liza yell so loudly.

"I can't believe Coach Graves didn't stop us," Howie muttered.

Melody nodded. "I wish she'd wake up and help us like she did last practice."

"She was great!" Howie agreed. "She was yelling directions and cheering us on. Now, she's just sitting there."

"Maybe she lost her voice from all that yelling," Liza suggested.

"Her voice was fine when she was talking to that witchy woman," Eddie reminded them. "Now, she's acting like a zombie from a late movie."

Melody's eyes got big. "You're right," she said slowly. "There's something wrong with Coach Graves, and I know what it is."

"What?" her friends asked at once.

Melody looked at each of them before speaking. "Gather round, and I'll tell you."

6
Huddle

Eddie, Liza, Melody, and Howie huddled close while the rest of the team dribbled the ball back down the field.

"What's wrong with the coach?" Eddie asked.

Melody put her fingers to her lips. "It's important that Coach Graves doesn't hear us," Melody warned softly. "People don't like finding out that they're zombies!"

"What are you talking about?" Liza gasped. "Coach Graves isn't a zombie."

Melody shook her head. "When I was visiting my cousin last summer, she told me some spooky things."

"What did she say?" Howie asked.

"She told me about an enchantress who could turn people into walking automatons."

"Like robots?" Eddie giggled.

"Sort of," Melody continued. "They were people put into a trance. They had to do whatever the enchantress wanted. These zombies couldn't look people in the eye and moved very slowly."

"What does all this have to do with Coach Graves?" Howie asked.

Melody rolled her eyes. "Must I tell you everything? That old lady put a spell on the coach and turned her into a zombie!"

Eddie grabbed Melody's arms and shook her. "I think you're the zombie and your brains have taken a permanent vacation."

"Eddie's right." Liza giggled. "After all, zombies don't play soccer."

"Besides," Howie added, "there is no such thing as zombies."

Eddie nodded. "Zombies are just made-up creatures in the movies."

Melody pointed to Coach Graves. "Then you won't mind marching up to

her and staring her straight in the eyes."

"Is that a dare?" Eddie asked.

Melody nodded. "It's a double dare."

Eddie marched away from his friends without looking back. He knew Liza, Melody, and Howie would follow him.

Eddie stopped right in front of Coach Graves and stared. The coach looked away. Eddie sidestepped so he was standing where she stared. Coach Graves looked to the left of him. Eddie hopped in front of her. This time, Coach Graves looked at the ground.

"I told you so," Melody hissed.

Eddie looked over his shoulder. He hated it when Melody was right. He kicked his toe into the dirt as he tried to think of a plan.

Eddie faced the coach again. "We're finished playing," he said. "It's time to go home. Do you want the ball back?"

Coach Graves stood up and walked with her arms held straight out. Slowly,

she walked. Step by step. Eddie's eyes grew bigger as Coach Graves came closer and closer, her long fingers reaching toward him. Eddie did the only thing he could . . . run!

7
Danger

Eddie leaned against the rough bark of the giant oak tree and gulped air. His three friends were right beside him.

"Eddie, I thought you didn't believe in zombies," Melody panted. "I've never seen you run so fast."

Liza stumbled to the ground and took giant breaths. "I don't know why we were running."

"Didn't you see the way Coach Graves was coming after Eddie?" Melody shrieked.

"She wasn't after Eddie," Howie interrupted, pointing across the playground. "She was just reaching for the ball."

Sure enough, Coach Graves bent down to get the ball. Then she turned and plodded across the field, heading down

Forest Lane. She hadn't gone far when the old woman stepped from the shadows of a scraggly crab apple tree.

"I bet she's giving Coach Graves an order," Melody whispered.

Howie shook his head. "You have no proof that Coach Graves is a zombie."

"Howie's right," Liza agreed. "You shouldn't be saying such horrible things about that old lady, even if she is scary-looking. Maybe she's Coach Graves's grandmother."

"But what if she did turn the coach into a zombie?" Eddie asked. "We could all be in danger. I bet zombies kill people just for the fun of it."

Melody shook her head so hard her pigtails slapped her on the nose. "Zombies aren't dangerous, unless you make them mad."

"Then Eddie's in big trouble," Liza giggled. "He makes everybody mad."

Eddie's face turned bright red. "I do not.

Besides, I'm not afraid of any zombie!"

"Good," Melody said. "Then you won't be afraid to follow her home."

"What?" Liza, Howie, and Eddie said at once.

Melody took a deep breath. "We have to find out for sure if Coach Graves is a zombie," she told her friends. "The whole city's safety may depend on it!"

8
Cemetery

"This place is creepy," Liza complained.

"Shhh," Melody hissed. "She'll hear you." The four friends had followed Coach Graves all the way past the Bailey City Cemetery to a tiny house. They were hiding in a huge pile of wood, watching their new coach dig a hole. Coach Graves slowly shoveled out a pile of dirt and tossed it over her shoulder. The dirt mound behind her grew bigger and bigger.

"What's she doing anyway?" Eddie asked.

"I don't know, but my mom is going to be mad," Howie said. "I should have been home an hour ago."

Melody dropped her backpack onto the

ground and sat on it. "I can't help it if Coach Graves walks slow."

"Slow!" Eddie said. "A snail is slow, the coach is . . ."

"A zombie," Melody said. "Look!"

The four kids watched as their coach threw the soccer ball into the hole she just dug. Then without a sound, she walked off.

"She threw away the team ball!" Howie said.

"Why would she do that?" Liza asked. "She loves soccer."

Melody stood up to watch Coach Graves walk away. "That witchy woman didn't want the coach to stay in Bailey City to help us with soccer. I bet she ordered Coach Graves to throw away our soccer ball. She's doing what the old woman told her!"

"I don't care about that old woman," Eddie said. "But I do care about the team ball. I'm going to get it."

"Are you crazy?" Liza squealed. "Do you know what that hole is?"

Eddie shook his head and hopped over the pile of wood.

"It's a grave," Howie said slowly. "It makes sense. Coach Graves was digging a grave."

Eddie gulped and looked into the deep hole. Howie was right, it was just the size

for a coffin. Eddie looked at his friends, then back into the hole again. He didn't want them to think he was afraid, but he didn't really want to jump in a grave. He shuddered.

"Don't do it," Liza whimpered.

Eddie stood on the edge of the deep hole. "Don't be silly," he told them. He sounded braver than he felt. "It's just a

hole." Eddie took a deep breath and closed his eyes. Then he jumped.

He landed right beside the soccer ball. "I've got it," Eddie said, quickly scooping up the ball. Then he reached up to pull himself out of the grave.

"Oh, no!" Eddie shouted. "It's too deep. I can't get out!"

Liza looked like she was about to faint, but Melody jumped over the woodpile and stuck her hand down inside the hole. "Come on, I'll help you," she said. Eddie stretched and tried to reach Melody's hand.

"Hurry!" Howie squealed. "Coach Graves is coming back!"

9
Breaking the Spell

The next afternoon Liza, Melody, Howie, and Eddie met under the oak tree on the school playground. Liza was still upset about what had happened in the back of Coach Graves' house. "I thought you were both goners," she told Eddie and Melody.

Howie sat down on the ground. "I don't know what would have happened if Coach Graves had seen you in that hole."

"But she didn't," Eddie pointed out. "Everything worked out just fine. I've got the team ball right here."

"But it's not going to work out if we don't break the spell that old lady has over the coach," Melody told them. "Don't forget our first game with the Sheldon

45

Shooters is in two days. We need Coach Graves or we're Shooter soup."

"What can we do?" Liza whimpered. "The Shooters are going to cream us!"

"We have to break the spell," Melody said firmly.

"But how?" Howie asked.

"Don't worry," Eddie said, heading over to the soccer field for practice. "I'm an expert at breaking things."

The four kids ran over to the field. It was just like yesterday. Coach Graves sat on the bleachers, staring into space.

"She looks like my mom after a hard day at work." Howie giggled.

Liza sat on the ground and adjusted her shin guards. "Maybe she's sleepwalking," Liza suggested.

"I'll change that," Eddie said. He ran up to the coach and jumped up and down. He made faces and stuck out his tongue.

Melody shook her head. "It's going to

take more than that to break a zombie spell."

"Let me try," Howie said. He snapped his fingers in the coach's face. Coach Graves just stared. She didn't even blink.

"I have an idea," Liza said, "but I don't think we should do it."

"This is an emergency," Melody told her. "We have to try anything that might make her snap out of it."

"Okay," Liza said. "We'll tickle her!"

"We can't just walk up to a zombie and tickle her," Melody said.

"But tickling always wakes me up," Liza explained.

Eddie nodded. "Liza's right. Whenever I tickle Grandma she shoots right out of her bed. I've never seen an old lady move so fast. If anything can cure a sleeping zombie, tickling can."

"*No!*" Melody screamed. "You might make her mad!"

But it was too late. Liza rushed over
and tickled Coach Graves under her chin.

Coach Graves stood up slowly.

"All right!" Eddie shouted. "You did it!"

Coach Graves groaned, shook her
head, then walked slowly off the soccer
field with her arms stretched out in front
of her.

"I didn't do it," Liza said sadly.

"That's okay," Howie said, patting her

on the back. "It was a good idea."

"I have another idea," Melody said. "And if it works, the only zombies around here will be the Sheldon Shooters after we beat them."

10
Peanut of an Idea

Liza and Howie watched Eddie crunch a bright yellow leaf under the heel of his dirty sneaker. It was the next day and they were huddled under their favorite oak tree on the playground waiting for soccer practice to start. Howie tore open a bag of his favorite snack. He offered some of the garlic-flavored potato chips to his friends.

"No, thanks," Liza said politely.

"Those things are horrible!" Eddie told Howie. "I don't know how you can stand to eat them. Didn't you bring something better?"

Just then, Melody walked across the playground carrying a big jar of peanuts.

"Now that's what I call a snack!" Eddie reached for the jar.

"Not so fast," Melody said, yanking the peanuts away. "These aren't for us. They're for Coach Graves. They're going to cure her."

"Your brain must have turned to peanut butter overnight." Eddie giggled. "There isn't anything wrong with Coach Graves."

"Not according to my cousin," Melody warned. "Mom let me call her last night. My cousin said we have to help Coach Graves right away, or we could all be in trouble. According to her, peanuts are just what we need."

"How can a jar of peanuts cure a zombie?" Howie asked.

"Simple." Melody grinned. "Everybody knows that salt cures zombies."

"I didn't know that," Liza said.

"Well, now you do," Melody told her.

Eddie pointed at the jar in Melody's hands. "That's a jar of peanuts. You said it took salt to cure a zombie."

Melody rolled her eyes. "Must I do all the thinking for you? You can't just walk up to a zombie and shake salt in her mouth."

"That's true." Liza nodded. "But where do the peanuts come in?"

"Peanuts have salt!" Melody snapped. "Don't you people know anything? According to my cousin, all we need is for Coach Graves to eat these salty peanuts, and our zombie troubles will be over!"

"I hope you're right," Howie sighed. "Tomorrow's our game with the Sheldon Shooters, and we need Coach Graves to win."

Eddie laughed. "We don't need anybody to win. Especially Coach Graves."

Liza put her hands on her hips. "You won't be so smug tomorrow with the

Sheldon Shooters slamming soccer balls into your stomach!"

"Liza's right," Howie interrupted. "We have to do something."

"And this is just the answer." Melody held up the jar of peanuts. "Let's go cure a zombie!"

11
Salt Free

Melody marched down the sideline and stopped right in front of Coach Graves. "I brought you a snack," she said, holding out the peanuts. "Want some?"

"No, thank you." Coach Graves spoke in a flat voice, almost like a moan.

"But you have to eat some," Melody told her. "They're good for you."

"Not hungry," Coach Graves mumbled.

"Just try a few peanuts," Melody suggested. "Then we can play soccer."

Coach Graves barely nodded, but she held out her hand and let Melody shake a few peanuts into her palm. Then she popped them in her mouth and chewed. Melody held her breath, but nothing happened. Coach Graves blinked once, but that was all.

"I thought you said peanuts would cure the coach," Liza whispered.

"My cousin told me salt would do the trick," Melody sniffed. "It's the only thing that cures zombies. I don't know what went wrong!"

"Let me see something," Howie said. He handed Melody his potato chip bag so he could take her peanut jar. "Here's the problem," he told them.

The three friends crowded close to see

where Howie pointed. There in big red letters it said *Salt Free.*

"Smooth move, peanut butter brain." Eddie laughed. "Did you forget how to read?"

"Leave her alone," Liza told him. "Everybody makes mistakes."

"Besides, we don't have time to argue," Howie warned. "It's time to practice."

The rest of the team was waiting for them, so Melody dropped Howie's potato chips on the bench next to Coach Graves and jogged onto the field. Liza, Howie, and Eddie followed her.

"This is our last practice before the big game," Melody said, grabbing the ball from Huey. "So listen to me and I'll tell you what to do."

Huey snatched the ball back. "We don't have to listen to you!"

"Melody does know more about soccer than the rest of us," Liza said. "Maybe she can give us some pointers."

"She's not the coach," Huey said. "We should do what the coach says."

"Who needs a coach?" Eddie interrupted. "Let's just play ball!" Then he bopped the ball out of Huey's hands and kicked it down the field.

The entire team chased the ball, but Eddie got to it first. He kicked, but he missed and his foot kicked air. He ended up sitting down hard on the ground. Nobody had time to laugh, because Melody swooped over to the ball and dribbled it down the field. Huey could only think of one way to stop her. He dove at her feet and tackled her to the ground.

"No fair!" Melody screamed.

Nobody listened, because they were already chasing after the soccer ball. Howie was almost to the ball when Liza darted in front of it. Liza sent the ball sailing down the field.

Howie screamed. "You kicked it the wrong way!"

That started everybody yelling. Melody shoved Huey and Eddie pushed everybody who got in his way.

"Stop!" Howie stood in the middle of the field, yelling loud enough for everyone to hear. "Huey was right. We should listen to Coach Graves."

The rest of the team glanced over to the bleachers. Coach Graves stared right through them, as if she didn't see a thing.

"How can we listen to her when she doesn't talk to us?" Eddie snapped.

"She tried to teach us," Liza said softly. "We just wouldn't listen."

Howie nodded. "We should play like Coach Graves taught us. She told us to remember that teamwork wins games. It's our only chance at winning against the Sheldon Shooters."

"Do you think it's possible?" Melody asked.

"Anything is possible," Howie said softly. "Even zombies."

So the Bailey Boomers practiced together all afternoon, trying to play just as Coach Graves had taught them. After two hours they were exhausted and ready to go home. As they straggled from the field, Howie stopped his friends. "I have to get my potato chips," he said.

Eddie, Liza, and Melody waited for their friend to grab the bag from the bleachers. Howie crumpled the empty bag. "Who ate my potato chips?" he grumbled.

"Not me," Liza said.

"I wouldn't touch those yucky things," Eddie told him.

Melody pointed. "There's the potato chip culprit."

The four friends looked just in time to see Coach Graves pop the last chip into her mouth.

12
Wake the Dead

The next day the kids were on the field at one o'clock sharp in their bright blue Bailey Boomers uniforms. Their knees started shaking when the Sheldon Shooters trotted onto the field in their black and gold uniforms.

"They're huge!" Liz squealed.

"They're elephants!" Howie gulped.

"We're dead," Eddie said, shaking his head.

Melody put her hands on her hips. "Don't talk like that! We're just as good as they are. Let's go out there and show those Shooters how to play soccer!"

"All right!" the Boomers yelled. Melody got the opening kick, but that was the last time the Boomers saw the ball. The Shooters scored two goals right away.

"I guess we really showed them," Eddie told Melody at halftime.

"We need the coach," Huey complained and rubbed a sore ankle. "They're running all over us."

The kids looked at the coach. She was sitting on the bleachers staring into space.

Melody shook her head. "We've tried everything. She even ate Howie's salty chips."

"Not everything," Liza said, taking a drink of water.

"What's left?" Eddie asked.

"Remember how the coach said that soccer is exciting enough to wake the dead?" Liza asked.

Howie, Melody, Eddie, and the rest of the team nodded their heads. "Well," said Liza, "let's wake her up! Let's play like we've never played before!"

"All right!" the team hollered and raced back onto the field. The Bailey Boomers got the ball and headed toward their goal. Eddie passed it to Melody.

"Go for it!" Liza screamed.

Melody zipped past a huge Sheldon Shooters player and kicked the ball into the goal.

"All right!" Howie shouted. "We're doing it!" He looked over to the bleacher. For a minute, he thought he saw Coach Graves smiling. But when he looked again, she was staring off into space.

"Let's go!" Eddie hollered as the Shooters kicked the ball back into play.

Melody stole the ball and dribbled it toward the goal, but she was quickly surrounded by huge Sheldon Shooters players.

"Pass it!" Howie screamed.

Melody booted the ball to Huey and, with one strong kick, Huey knocked the ball past the goalie and scored. Now it was 2–2.

"Yes!" Liza screamed and the whole

team jumped up and down. Liza looked at the bleachers. The coach was clapping. But before Liza had a chance to tell anybody, play started again.

Melody stole the ball again, but this time a huge Sheldon Shooters player stuck his foot out in front of her. "No fair!" Eddie shouted. "That's tripping!"

Melody fell to the ground and didn't get up. The referee whistled for a free kick. "Are you all right?" Liza asked.

Melody shook her head. "I think I twisted my ankle. You'll have to finish the game without me."

"We can't do it without you!" Huey told her. "You're our best player."

Melody smiled. "Yes, you can. Just remember what the coach told you about teamwork."

The Boomers nodded their heads and helped Melody off the field. In just a few seconds, the Shooters almost scored a

Boomers! Just wait until our next practice. We'll practice so hard, those other teams won't stand a chance."

Melody, Liza, Howie, and Eddie looked at each other. "Uh-oh," Liza whispered. "Maybe we should have left her a zombie!"

Debbie Dadey and Marcia Thornton Jones have fun writing stories together. When they both worked at an elementary school in Lexington, Kentucky, Debbie was the school librarian and Marcia was a teacher. During their lunch break in the school cafeteria, they came up with the idea of the Bailey School kids.

Recently Debbie and her family moved to Plano, Texas. Marcia and her husband still live in Kentucky where she continues to teach. How do these authors still write together? They talk on the phone and use computers and fax machines!

Creepy, weird, wacky and
funny things happen to
the Bailey School Kids!™
Collect and read them all!

The Adventures of
THE BAILEY SCHOOL KIDS®